TRUTH UNFOLDS (MY SPIRITUAL QUEST)

BISWAJEET SRKR

This book is lovingly dedicated to my father, Pradip Sarkar. His unwavering support, guidance, and motivation have been the cornerstone of my life and spiritual journey.

He instilled a deep sense of purpose and a quest for truth from my early years. His wisdom has encouraged me to seek answers beyond the material world, and his love has given me the strength to overcome life's challenges.

I offer this humble work to him and all those seeking to discover the deeper meaning of existence. It may serve as a stepping stone toward finding the truth within.

Contents

Foreword

In today's fast-paced world, where distractions arise constantly, and life's complexities grow daily, many of us feel a deep longing for meaning, clarity, and peace. We seek a path that transcends the noise and leads us to the core of our existence, where Truth resides. Truth Unfolds (My Spiritual Quest) recounts a journey of spiritual discovery, inner awakening, and self-realization.

The inspiration behind this book comes from an intense quest to understand life beyond its material dimensions. This journey is not unique to the author alone but is shared by countless individuals worldwide who feel a calling toward something greater than themselves. As you turn these pages, you will find personal experiences intertwined with spiritual teachings, illuminating the path toward realizing your true self.

What makes this book special is its simplicity and authenticity. The author's honest recounting of his challenges and realizations makes it a relatable and inspiring read. It encourages readers to explore their spiritual path without dictating a specific direction or imposing dogma. Instead, it offers wisdom and tools to help navigate the complexities of modern life with a spiritual compass. This book does not promise easy solutions but provides insights that may transform your thinking.

For those beginning their spiritual journey, Truth Unfolds (My Spiritual Quest) is an excellent companion, reminding us that spirituality is not about perfection but about progress, no matter how small. For seasoned seekers, it reaffirms that the journey to Truth is ongoing, and each step brings us closer to the divine within. I invite you to explore this book with an open heart and mind. May it inspire you to find your path and unfold the Truth within you.

Preface

Spirituality has always fascinated me, as it does for many people navigating the complexities of modern life. I spent years seeking answers in various places, trying to understand the deeper meanings behind reality and the universe. For a long time, I struggled with the distractions of the material world, feeling detached from my inner self, overwhelmed by life's pressures, and searching for peace.

Truth Unfolds (My Spiritual Quest) results from my quest for peace and clarity. It is not a traditional guide to spirituality, nor does it offer a step-by-step solution to life's challenges. Instead, this book is an honest reflection of my spiritual journey—a journey shaped by teachings, scriptures, personal experiences, and the guidance of Shree Bhakti Purusottama Swami, whose work Who Am I profoundly influenced my understanding of spiritual truth.

In this book, I explore the real essence of spirituality—not as something practiced for show or material gain, but as a way of life. I share how chanting the holy name of Lord Krishna has transformed my life, making even the most difficult tasks more manageable and filling me with an inner sense of peace. Through my experiences, I have understood that spirituality is not a destination to be reached but a constant journey that requires sincerity, patience, and an open heart.

I dedicate this work to my father, Pradip Sarkar, whose love and support have been my guiding light. His wisdom has always encouraged me to seek the truth, and I am eternally grateful for his presence in my life. I offer this book as a small contribution to the broader spiritual conversation and hope it will inspire you to reflect on your journey. Let this be a starting point for your quest as you discover the spiritual truths within you.

Acknowledgements

Writing Truth Unfolds (My Spiritual Quest) has been a deeply personal and transformative journey. While I embarked on this path alone, the knowledge of Shree Bhakti Purusottama Swami profoundly shaped my inspiration. His teachings opened my heart to the true meaning of spirituality and guided me in unfolding the layers of my spiritual quest.

I sincerely thank Shree Bhakti Purusottama Swami for his illuminating book, 'Who Am I?' His work motivated me to reflect on my journey and pen down my thoughts. Through his insights, I found clarity and direction, for which I am forever grateful.

To my readers, thank you for accompanying me on this spiritual exploration. I hope this book resonates with you and offers guidance as you continue your quest for Truth and self-discovery.

Prologue

In a world where material pursuits often outweigh the spiritual, we search for a more profound sense of meaning and purpose. My journey has been one of continuous inquiry, self-reflection, and discovery, guided by the divine presence of Lord Krishna and the wisdom imparted through chanting His holy name.

Truth Unfolds (My Spiritual Quest) reflects my spiritual awakening—a journey that began with a quest for answers to profound questions about existence, purpose, and the nature of the soul. Through sacred texts, spiritual teachers, and introspection, I began to unfold the layers of truth that had always been present but obscured by the distractions of daily life.

This book is not a manual for enlightenment or a roadmap to spiritual perfection. Instead, it offers insights and reflections on spirituality as I understand it—an ongoing process of growth and discovery. The chapters speak to the essence of mindfulness, the power of chanting, and the value of connecting with the divine nature within ourselves and all living beings.

I dedicate this work to those seeking to rise above the illusions of the material world and those yearning for a connection with something more significant. My experiences, rooted in the teachings of Lord Krishna and inspired by the works of Shree Bhakti Purusottama Swami, form the foundation of this quest.

May the following pages inspire you to explore your spiritual path, to question, reflect, and discover the truth that unfolds within you.

CHAPTER ONE

INTRODUCTION

In a world filled with distractions and complexities, we often seek a more profound meaning and experiences. Truth Unfolds (My Spiritual Quest) mirrors my journey toward self-discovery and spirituality, motivated by profound teachings and personal experiences. This book aims to illuminate the path to realizing our true essence, transcending the material and mental realms.

As we navigate the challenges of everyday life, it's easy to lose sight of our spiritual connection. Yet, this connection grounds us, offering clarity and purpose. My journey has been one of learning, unlearning, and rediscovering the essence of who we are beyond societal labels and expectations. The purpose of this book is to spread proper spiritual knowledge everywhere. No one should be misguided by any fraud who knows nothing about spirituality.

This book will help people overcome their challenges through appropriate spiritual understanding, encouraging readers to question preconceived notions and explore the depths of their beliefs. I dedicate this book to my father, Mr.Pradip Sarkar, whose tireless support and love have been instrumental in my life.

His wisdom and guidance have encouraged me to seek truth and understanding, shaping my spiritual journey. May this work serve as a guide, inspiring you to embark on your path of self-discovery and a more profound connection with the universe.

CHAPTER TWO

The Silent Warnings

The silent warning comes from the Soul & Supersoul.

Life is easy until we make it difficult. I have experienced this many times, and you can observe it in daily life. A simple task becomes complicated when we delay it until the last minute. Every day, someone creates this kind of mess. I do, too. If it were limited to small tasks, it would be manageable. But we often carry these bad habits into more significant areas of our lives—where the real problem begins.

Now, I want to share an incident that shows exactly how I could have avoided a major problem by making the right decision. In 2022, I joined a new company, upgrading my professional role. I was adjusting well to the new work culture and enjoying the job.

Everything was going smoothly until, at the end of the year, I received a call from my previous company, where I had worked for more than five years. The call was from a senior colleague whom I respected greatly. I use "respected" because I learned a lot from him. He offered me the chance to return to the company.

What would you do if you were in my situation? You had just switched jobs a year ago, and things in your current company were going well. I assume most people would say something like, "I'll think about it, Sir." Even an intelligent person would respond that way. But I lost my sense of judgment at that moment.

Without thinking, I said, "Okay, please proceed." I didn't want to say no because I thought it would be disrespectful. I rejoined the company. No, I didn't just rejoin—I actually invited trouble for myself. The workplace I returned to was the worst environment I had ever experienced. Each day was a struggle. After a year, I left that company again, earning myself the label of a 'frequent job-changer.'

But I don't blame anyone for this situation. In fact, I even thanked the senior who had recommended me for the role. It wasn't his team, but still, he suggested my name for the position. The only person I could blame was myself for not making the right decision. I consider it a big mistake because it was not just about a minor task—it involved my career.

Now, let me share a recent incident, one that didn't just impact a career but several lives. This incident will show how one wrong decision can ruin not just one life but four. There was a 29-year-old boy, a loving son of his parents. I know him well because he was my cousin. He got everything he ever wanted from his parents, and this constant indulgence became a harmful habit.

This indulgence led him into drug addiction. He used all kinds of drugs. Stealing money and disrespecting his parents became his daily routine. Eventually, fed up with his behavior, his parents sent him to a rehabilitation center. While there, he fell in love with a girl living with her aunt. The girl was simple and innocent.

They eloped and got married. Later, they had a daughter. But despite all this, he couldn't free himself from addiction. His situation worsened, and his health deteriorated. Slowly, his body broke down, heading toward death. One early morning, his soul left his body. Now, his once-happy parents live childless, his wife is a widow, and his daughter is fatherless.

But the real question is: why are these four lives suffering? Actually, no—that's the wrong question. The real question should be: why is the innocent baby girl suffering? If his parents had made the right decision early on, they could have steered their son away from addiction. If the girl had made the right decision, she might not have fallen in love with him.

Yes, it's all about making the right decisions. It's about going in the right direction. Have you ever thought, "I wish something could stop me from making mistakes?" We all want that. But do you know that something inside us does give us repeated warnings? That "something" is the soul and the Supersoul within us. They give us hints, but we often don't listen.

Think about my cousin's story. In his body, where two pure entities—the soul and Supersoul—dwelt, he tortured himself and made his body filthy. He received silent warnings from his soul and the Supersoul—urging him to return to the right path—but he never responded.

He made his body uninhabitable for these pure entities. Ultimately, they couldn't remain in such a defiled body. There must have been many silent conversations between the soul, the Supersoul, the body, and the mind. Those silent warnings indeed passed through these conversations. I have described those conversations in my own words. I hope you'll understand.

The Soul is not active anymore,
Polluted by money, greed, and obscenity.
    It cries for help from the Supersoul,
Yelling,
"Oh Lord, please save me from this illusion," the Soul pleads.
    "Wait and don't worry; let's give your body a chance,"
The Supersoul replies.
    They begin to give hints—
Hints to return,
Return to the real.
    "These are all fleeting pleasures;
Please come back," says the Supersoul.
    The body did not listen to the mind,
And the mind did not listen to the Soul.
    Both got distracted by illusion,
Captured by inferior energy.
    For many years, it went on like this.
Smoke and alcohol filled the bloodstream.
    The body coughed all day,
Short of breath.
    The Soul couldn't find space to breathe.
Eosinophil counts dropped. "Don't worry; nothing will happen.
Just keep going," said the mind.
    But one day, the body and mind fell numb.
They both lay on the bed, waiting.
    "Waiting for the moment
When I'll leave this body," said the Soul.
    Finally, the day came.
The body and mind stopped responding.
The Supersoul took the Soul, leaving the body behind.
    "If only you had listened to us,
Maybe we could have spent more days together,"
The Supersoul whispered as they departed.

BLAMING THE INNOCENT

Whenever we blame the soul, we blame the innocent.

People always like to blame others. It is very natural nowadays in this community. But it fits as long as people blame something non-living.

Suppose I purchased a pair of Fast-Track sunglasses, and suddenly, they broke. Or the video quality of my new Samsung phone could be better. If I blame Fast-Track and Samsung in these two cases, that would be justified.

However, we are not limited to blaming non-living entities. Blaming a living entity these days is very typical.

But do you know that when you blame a living entity, you are blaming an innocent?

Yes, this is true, and now I will prove it. I was unaware of this until I realized the truth after reading Shree Bhakti Purusottam Swami's book, Who Am I.

Let's explain this using a real example.

There was a man who married an abnormal girl. Though I say she is abnormal, she did all the domestic work, like cooking, washing, and cleaning. But her problem was that she had no analytical capability.

Suppose she was cooking; while doing it, she suddenly laughed. Or, you are busy with an urgent task, and just then, the girl says something to you. Since you are occupied, you do not answer her call.

Then the girl gets angry with you. She stops talking and starts to cry because you hadn't spoken to her at that moment.

This situation becomes very dull for you. You start to wonder what you did wrong. If you express your anger towards her, the girl will become even angrier. It's possible to calm her only by caressing her.

As the girl used to do all the work for her family, it would not be right to call her abnormal. Her brain, unfortunately, especially disabled her. But her parents loved her very much; she belonged to a middle-class family.

As the girl grew older, her parents' worries increased. They wanted their daughter to marry someone very responsible and sincere. They had another wish: their daughter should always be near them.

For that, they agreed to build a new house for their daughter and her husband.

They searched and found a boy. The boy agreed to marry her and took a dowry of 51,000 rupees. As promised, the girl's parents built a new house.

However, the man showed his true nature after marriage. He started drinking alcohol every day, beat her, and demanded money from his in-laws. After enduring so much torture, the girl loved the man very much.

Then, one day, the man left the girl alone. Perhaps he married someone else.

After witnessing all these incidents, people in the girl's neighborhood made many nasty comments about the man.

I did too, as I am the girl's cousin. Some people said the man was an impure soul, so he was doing these wrong things.

But after reading Sri Bhakti Purusottama Swami's book, I realized that we were all wrong. A soul can never be impure. His body and mind were directed by inferior energy, which led to the actions he took.

In this case, the Holy Spirit is innocent.

When we blame any living entity, we directly blame the Soul. But the truth is that the Soul is always innocent. If we do something wrong, inferior energy is the reason behind it.

This inferior energy is the key to the illusion. Our body and mind act according to what this energy dictates, and we are neither the body nor the mind.

CHAPTER FOUR

THE ONE WITHIN ALL

The Soul and Supersoul are present in every living entity.

We hear from our elders that God resides in children, and I accepted this as reality. As kids are pure and divine, people associate children with the presence of God.

However, after reading the book by Shree Bhakti Purusottama Swami, I see this as a myth. Approximately 385,000 babies are born each day. If God is in the children, can we assume God's number is 385,000?

Not possible. You may have also heard that God exists in all living beings. But tell me, how is that true How can God cut Himself into pieces and give these parts to all living entities?

Actually, we, including children, are fragmental parts of the Supersoul or Paramatma. We are the superior energy of the Supersoul. As fragmental parts, the Supersoul is present in every living entity.

The scripture Bhagavad Gita and the book Who Am I refer to this truth. While children are pure and innocent, the same fragment of divinity exists in adults.

As we age, we slowly come into contact with illusion and its inferior energy. Then distraction appears, and we start to damage our bodies.

Instead of saying our body is impure, we claim the Soul is impure. But the truth is that the Soul is always pure and fresh.

Yes, the Soul remains pure even as we grow older. However, spiritual purity is about connecting with the Supersoul regardless of age.

Just a few days ago, I saw a video on Facebook. In the video, a child was playing in the garden when, suddenly, a ferocious dog came to attack him.

The dog was so fierce that it could have harmed the child severely. But a miracle happened: the child's pet dog appeared and saved him. This incident shows that the Supersoul exists within all beings, not just children.

It reminds us that while external differences may exist, all living entities are connected through the Supersoul. If we can free ourselves from the inferior energy of illusion, we can receive lifelong blessings from the Soul and Supersoul.

We all have divine potential because the divine spark resides within us. This spark helps us live in alignment with our true purpose and allows us to grow spiritually.

One thing became clear to me after visiting the ISKCON temple: our connection to the divine depends on our actions, known as Karma. Our Karma directly influences our spiritual journey.

Always view our connection to the divine as a spiritual bridge. Our body and mind are tools to maintain this bridge. By caring for our body (through health, diet, exercise, or yoga) and mind (through meditation, focus, and devotion), we strengthen this bridge and enhance our spiritual journey.

As I mentioned before, the Supersoul is present in all living entities. Therefore, we must show respect to all living creatures, recognizing the presence of the One within all.

BEYOND WORSHIP: UNDERSTANDING GOD

There is something beyond worship.

The book Who Am I is fantastic. This is the first time I gained so many insights into self-existence and God from a single book. I was so confident that I could participate in any discussion on God and self-existence. One day, I decided to test my knowledge from the book. My mother was resting after finishing her work. Although I had finished the book, I was still reading the first chapter. My mother showed interest in the book and suddenly started a conversation.

"What are you reading, my son?" my mother asked. "A spiritual book," I replied. "What is this book about?" she inquired.

"It's about spirituality and self-existence," I said. "Wow, the cover page is very attractive! Can you please tell me more about this book?" she asked.

Feeling a bit distracted, I said, "Maa, please let me read." My mother stubbornly persisted, saying, "You have to explain."

Finally, I surrendered and said okay. I started the summary by asking her a question. "Maa, first you tell me, who are you?" I asked. She didn't take a second to reply with her name.

"Don't be in a hurry; think a little more," I encouraged. "A human being," my mother answered.

"Maa, please think for a minute and then answer," I said. Then she got angry and said, "I asked you to explain, and you are asking me."

"Leave it. I don't want anything from you," she added.

"Maa, relax. I am explaining, and this question is part of it. You can see that this question is also the title of this book," I clarified.

"Okay," she said. After taking a pause, she replied, "Maybe I am a human body." I then asked my mother another question.

"Okay, now tell me, I see that you worship God daily. What do you do during worship?" I inquired. "I pray to God for my family's good health and wealth," she said.

"Okay, Maa, you told me you are just a body, right?" I asked. She confirmed with a yes.

"Now, suppose a boy is playing with his grandmother, as he does every day. Afterward, he goes to school. When he returns, he sees his grandmother lying on the bed. He moves closer to her, and she loves him dearly. Then, he goes out to play with his friends.

When he returns after playing, he sees a crowd gathered around his grandmother, all crying.

He asks his mother, 'What happened?' 'Your granny is no longer here, my son,' the boy's mother replies.

'But before I went to play, I saw my granny lying on the bed. Even now, she is lying on the bed. Why are you saying she is no longer here when I can see her right there?' the boy asks.

I posed the same question to my mother. She smiled and paused. Now, she asked me to answer. "I said that was not the body that died. If it was just the body, then why was the boy's mother saying his granny was no longer here? Am I right?" I asked.

"Yes," my mother replied. "If that was just the body, then why, after dying, can't she play with the boy anymore?" I asked again.

"Yes, then who was she?" my mother inquired. "That was the Soul," I explained. I then summarized the book and gave her a proper understanding. "Wow, I never thought of this before," my mother said.

In that moment, I realized that my mother had poor knowledge of God and self-existence, simply because no one had asked her these questions before. I acknowledge that worship, prayers, rituals, and temple visits are all necessary, but these are just the basics of a spiritual journey. To truly understand God, we need to go beyond these external actions and create an inner connection.

It's not simply a matter of worshipping with full awareness that will lead you to understand God. For that, you need to develop a pure, personal connection with the divine. This is possible through meditation, seeing God in the beauty of nature, or in acts of kindness. I feel there should be a theologian or guru for everyone who can provide this knowledge about the self and God.

CHAPTER SIX

CONVERSATIONS ON THE RAILS

Conversations on rails to find self itself-existence.

On 13th September 2024, I was traveling to Mumbai on the Agartala LTT Express. I boarded the train from New Jalpaiguri Station.

I moved to my seat and found a few people as my co-passengers who had boarded the train from Agartala.

What I thought about the people of Agartala proved true after seeing them. They are innocent, and you can find a sense of peace on their faces. I am also a Bengali, like them, but their language seems much sweeter.

I have a great habit of easily interacting with others, and I mixed with them effortlessly. They asked me about my hometown and workplace, and they shared that they were going on a pilgrimage.

They even offered me their food and addressed me as "son." Their behavior was very polite. A few of them were members of the ISKCON Temple, and some were chanting Lord Krishna's name.

Suddenly, a moment came when they started a discussion on self-existence and God. At that time, I was reading a book and got excited about their discussion.

Since I had recently finished the book Who Am I, I felt confident enough to participate. After seeing my enthusiasm in the discussion, someone asked me a question.

He inquired, "How do you know these things?" I replied, "This book is titled Who Am I by Shree Bhakti Purusottama Swami," and showed them the book on my phone.

That man said they knew the author. I was thrilled and exclaimed, "Wow!" "Yes, and he comes to Agartala every year," the man said.

The discussion picked up pace. One man who was also with them disagreed with the existence of God, while four agreed with the belief.

Suddenly, one of them asked my opinion on the matter. I smiled and shared my views from Who Am I.

"Yes, God exists," I stated, proving this with a few examples from the book. I also explained the concepts of the soul and the Supersoul using additional examples. Then, I received a cross-question: "Is Lord Krishna God?"

There, I found myself stuck, as my spiritual knowledge had its limitations. The answer should have been mentioned in the book, so I humbly admitted that I would need to research this further.

None of them could answer it either. I understood that it's a difficult question and that I would need to delve deeper into spirituality to find the answer. I told that man that I would soon find out the answer. They appreciated my knowledge and behavior.

I did not realize how quickly time passed with them. They got down at Nagpur Railway Station, and I helped them with their luggage. They shared their contact details with me.

One of them assured me he would arrange a meeting with Shree Bhakti Purusottama Swami in Agartala. I am incredibly excited to meet him. Just think about it—the man who can make someone spiritual just by reading a book. How capable he must be spiritually!

CHAPTER SEVEN

CHANTING FOR CLARITY

The secret of chanting for clarity.

I observe how the chanting of Lord Krishna's name creates a vibration inside me. Most of the time, I visit the ISKCON temple with my fiancée, and she also feels the same vibration. The beauty of the scene when everyone chants the following is unmatchable:

""Hare Krishna, Hare Krishna, Krishna Krishna Hare Hare;
Hare Rama, Hare Rama, Rama Rama Hare Hare.""

Even I have noticed that chanting makes my difficult tasks feel more accessible. This has not happened just once; I have observed it many times. I believe that in our Hindu tradition, this chanting plays a significant role.

It provides a feeling of peace. If you chant this in the morning, you will feel connected with God during your meditation.

Now, I chant whenever I get the time, and I encourage my readers to do the same. Visit the ISKCON temple, participate in the group chanting, and enjoy the peace. There is also a myth: people think that if you visit ISKCON and participate in Lord Krishna's chanting, you must give up non-vegetarian meals. I see this as a misconception.

I want to clarify that whenever your mind participates in chanting with full attention, you will naturally feel inclined to stop consuming non-veg on your own; no one will ask you to stop.

To understand the benefits of Lord Krishna, let me share an incident involving my colleague. I won't mention his name but will share the complete incident.

He is married and has a ten-year-old son. He had a love marriage, meaning he has a lovely family where he loves his wife very much. It's expected that the amount of love is greater in a love marriage than in an arranged marriage.

Since we both work in sales, we see each other very often and often talk on the phone. Just a few months ago, I noticed my colleague seemed depressed. I asked him, "What happened?"

"Nothing, I am fine," he replied.

I observed him shouting at someone on the phone while we were on the field, and I thought it was due to the heavy workload.

After a few days, he called me, and when I picked up, he shared everything. At first, he didn't want to say anything, but I assured him he might find a solution by sharing his problem.

He then revealed that he was involved in an extramarital affair. Yes, this was the case. After hearing this, I was shocked and speechless for a few seconds because I had no idea he could be involved in such things.

"I am apprehensive, friend; I didn't get into this knowingly," he said sadly.

There was a girl in his rented flat who had asked for his help with a few tasks. He helped her, and from that, a relationship formed.

It may sound strange, but it's true that he was having an extramarital affair. In the absence of his wife, he visited many places with that girl. My colleague's wife was absent because they were having a silent fight at the time.

However, after everything was resolved between him and his wife, he wasn't ready to continue that affair. That's when the problem began.

The girl was not willing to move on and started blackmailing him, which was the source of my colleague's tension. He didn't know how to handle the situation. After hearing all this, I gently advised him to convince the girl to move on.

"I have tried to convince her so many times, but she is not ready to listen," my colleague replied.

I suggested he share this with his wife as a big mistake. I said this because I was concerned for him; I didn't want him to make the wrong decision. His wife could help him get out of this.

"Friend, I will never get involved in these things again. I made a mistake. I will go to the ISKCON temple and share this with Lord Krishna. Now, only Lord Krishna can save me," he said.

He shared this with his wife. After that, she didn't speak to him for two long days. Meanwhile, the girl's torture continued.

My colleague started spending more time at the ISKCON temple, but his performance at work began to decline, reflecting poorly on his monthly sales results.

Then, a week later, I received another call from him. He was laughing loudly and shared good news with me.

"My friend, everything is sorted now. That girl called me and said not to contact her again. She is in a new relationship with someone else. I even verified this; I saw her with someone in a coffee shop," my colleague said.

"Wow, that's excellent news! Congratulations!" I exclaimed.

"Thank you! I think only Lord Krishna helped me here. I spent more time at the ISKCON temple during group chanting," my colleague replied.

After that incident, I saw him change significantly. He loves to engage with God most of the time. His son's birthday fell during this Durga Puja, and he was in Vrindavan.

I understood the benefits of chanting Lord Krishna's name during challenging situations, but it must come from a pure mind and heart.

I have my own definition of chanting. For me, chanting is not just about reciting the name of God; it's a way to concentrate. Most of the time, we get lost in outer thoughts or distractions, but chanting pulls us back to the present moment.

When I chant Lord Krishna's name, I try to visualize His face with my inner eyes. This practice calms my mind from external distractions, bringing a sense of coolness and peace. Remember, chanting is not about the time or duration but about the purity of your intent.

CHAPTER EIGHT

THE TRUTH BEHIND

There is a truth behind everything.

What do you know about your existence? Who are you? Who is God? Are you your body? Are you your mind? Does the Soul exist? Does the Soul die?

If you have answers to these questions, you understand the truth behind the mystery.

Unless you ask yourself these questions, you will remain unaware of the truth and may spread misinformation about your existence. I was also in the dark about this. But after reading the book Who Am I? by Shree Bhakti Purusottama, I cleared my doubts and learned the truth behind my existence.

After completing the book, I told my mother that my relationship with her is formed by this physical body and mind, not by my true self. Because I am not the body, and I am not the mind. Similarly, you can find all your answers by reading this book, Truth Unfolds (My Spiritual Quest). This book is a reflection of Who Am I? by Shree Bhakti Purusottama. By regularly chanting the name of Lord Krishna, you will create a connection with the Supersoul and with Lord Krishna.

If you are about to do something wrong, you will be alerted in advance by the Soul and Supersoul. Our lives can often feel normal and aimless, but they will gain direction only when you understand your existence. We always try to comprehend the existence of God, yet we rarely seek to understand our own existence. My book can serve as a lens for you—a lens of spirituality. This lens will help you discover the truth behind every life challenge.

After exploring yourself with this book, you will be free from fear—the fear of death, confusion, and uncertainty. We have a pure Soul within our hearts, and alongside this Soul, there exists the Supersoul. It is our responsibility to keep both of them pure, as they inherently are.

What must we do about this?

Nothing; we should lead a simple life by awakening our spirituality. We will not harm anyone, cheat anyone, or pollute our bodies through harmful activities such as smoking or consuming alcohol. You will receive direction from the Soul and Supersoul. I struggled with anger issues and made many mistakes in the past, like breaking my phone and insulting seniors.

But I've found a new direction since I started chanting Lord Krishna's name. We can avoid making mistakes by listening to the silent voice within. Nowadays, everyone is tempted by illusion and its inferior energy. Today's biggest distraction is our smartphones. This isn't just the truth—it's a bitter reality. Someone might call me a gyani baba, but I don't care because I'm not.

Through this book, I'm not insisting that you awaken your spirituality. That's up to you. I'm simply unfolding the truth of spirituality. Spirituality isn't about what you show when you worship. It's not about feeding a poor person while recording it on camera. And it's definitely not spiritual to chant God's name just to become prosperous or safe.

If chanting God's name made people rich, beggars wouldn't sit outside temples. Isn't that true? After reading the book by Shree Bhakti Purusottama Swami, I clearly understood something: spirituality is about loving every living entity. Spirituality is about genuinely connecting with your soul and the Supersoul.

Spirituality is not a destination; it is a continuous journey. Illusions will be there to create challenges in our lives. These will distract and tempt us. But it is our responsibility to stay connected with our divine presence. We always talk about our spiritual growth. But what do you understand about spiritual growth? Does it mean perfection?

No, it doesn't imply perfection. It's about progress—even if that progress is negligible. I am always grateful to Shree Bhakti Purusottama Swami for his fantastic book, Who Am I? It inspired me to write Truth Unfolds (My Spiritual Quest).

I hope you've enjoyed this journey. If even 1% of your spiritual understanding changes after reading this book, I will be successful. I will resume my spiritual journey from here, and I hope you will, too. Let the truths this book shares be stepping stones for your discovery. In the end, spirituality is personal; only you can unfold your truth.

Author's Note

Writing Truth Unfolds (My Spiritual Quest) has been a deeply personal and transformative journey. This book mirrors my quest for spiritual wisdom and the understanding I have gained. Through my experiences, I have learned that actual knowledge lies in looking beyond the material and focusing on the spiritual essence that connects us all.

The intent of this book is not just to share my story but to offer readers an opportunity to reflect on their paths. I have drawn inspiration from the teachings of ancient spiritual texts and my exploration into the depths of self-realization. This book will serve as a guide for anyone seeking clarity amidst the complexities of life.

As you turn these pages, I encourage you to approach this book with an open heart and mind. Whether you are just beginning your spiritual journey or are already on your path, may this work inspire reflection, deeper understanding, and peace.

Thank you for allowing me to be a part of your journey.

Biswajeet Srkr